MILITARY MACHINES

MILITARY HELICOPTERS

By Mark Harasymiw

Gareth Stevens
Publishing

Please visit our website, www.garethstevens.com. For a free color catalog of all our high-quality books, call toll free 1-800-542-2595 or fax 1-877-542-2596.

Library of Congress Cataloging-in-Publication Data

Harasymiw, Mark.
  Military helicopters / Mark Harasymiw.
      p. cm. — (Military machines)
  Includes index.
  ISBN 978-1-4339-8468-6 (pbk.)
  ISBN 978-1-4339-8469-3 (6-pack)
  ISBN 978-1-4339-8467-9 (library binding)
  1. Military helicopters—United States. I. Title.
  UG1233.H35 2013
  623.74'6047—dc23
                                                  2012028334

First Edition

Published in 2013 by
Gareth Stevens Publishing
111 East 14th Street, Suite 349
New York, NY 10003

Copyright © 2013 Gareth Stevens Publishing

Designer: Michael J. Flynn
Editor: Kristen Rajczak

Photo credits: Cover, p. 1 Kenny Swartout/US Navy/Getty Images; p. 4 Branger/Hulton Archive/Getty Images; p. 5 Hulton Archive/Getty Images; pp. 6–7 Keystone-France/Gamma-Keystone/Getty Images; courtesy of the US Air Force: pp. 8, 24, 25 by Senior Airman Julianne Showalter, 29; p. 9 courtesy of the US Coast Guard; courtesy of the US Army: pp. 10, 16–17, 20–21 by Sgt. 1st Class Eric Pahon, 23 , 28; p. 11 Dwight Smith/Shutterstock.com; pp. 12–13 Getty Images; p. 14 Alfred Batungbacal/Time & Life Pictures/Getty Images; p. 15 Rolls Press/Popperfoto/Getty Images; p. 19 courtesy of the US Navy by Mass Communication Specialist 3rd Class Robyn Gerstenslager; p. 27 Stocktrek Images/Getty Images.

Printed in the United States of America

CPSIA compliance information: Batch #CW13GS: For further information contact Gareth Stevens, New York, New York at 1-800-542-2595.

CONTENTS

Words in the glossary appear in **bold** type the first time they are used in the text.

EARLY HELICOPTERS

The idea for a machine like the helicopter has been around for hundreds of years. The famous artist Leonardo da Vinci drew plans for a helicopter in the 16th century!

Before a successful helicopter could be made, several problems had to be solved. First, early engines were too heavy. The invention of the internal combustion engine, which is the engine used to power cars, allowed the first helicopters to fly. However, early helicopters sometimes flipped over because their single **rotor** created too much **torque**. The first helicopters shook a lot and were hard to control, too.

Inventors all over the world experimented with different engines and rotor placement in helicopters during the late 1800s and early 1900s.

4

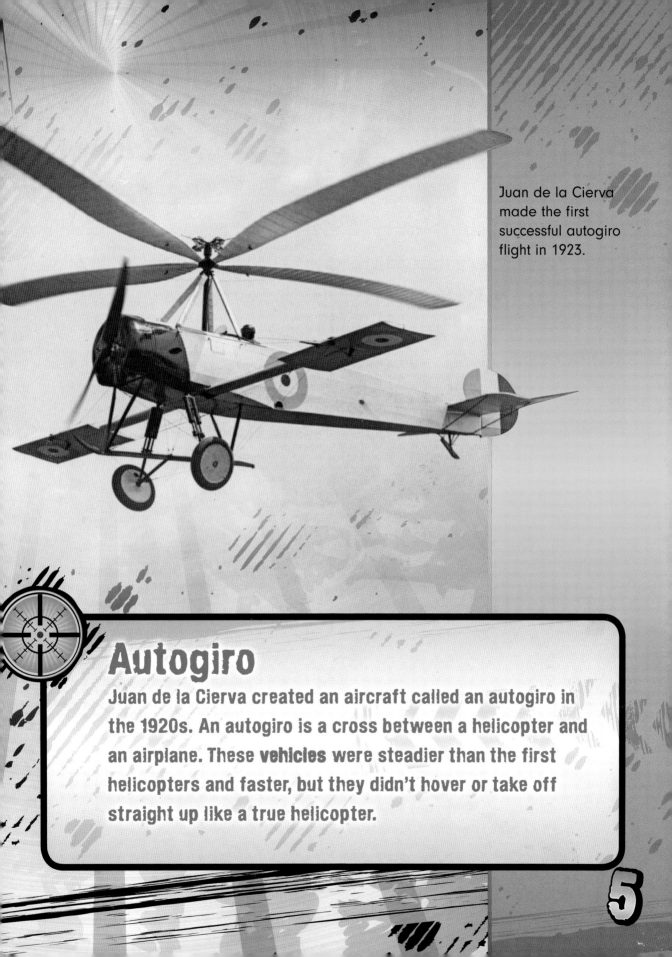

Juan de la Cierva made the first successful autogiro flight in 1923.

Autogiro

Juan de la Cierva created an aircraft called an autogiro in the 1920s. An autogiro is a cross between a helicopter and an airplane. These **vehicles** were steadier than the first helicopters and faster, but they didn't hover or take off straight up like a true helicopter.

SIKORSKY'S VS-300

Igor Sikorsky, a Russian who moved to the United States, **designed** one of the first successful helicopters—the VS-300. Today, many helicopters are still based on this model. Before Sikorsky designed the VS-300, he experimented for many years. His first designs in 1909 and 1910 failed because their engines weren't powerful enough.

In 1941, the VS-300 successfully flew for 1 hour and 32 minutes!

The VS-300's design solved the early helicopter's problem of flipping upside down. Sikorsky added a smaller rotor to the tail of the helicopter to spin in the opposite direction of the big rotor on top of the helicopter. It countered the torque and kept the helicopter right side up.

More Solutions

Other inventors found ways to solve the helicopter's troubles, too. Some built helicopters with two large rotors—one near the front of the helicopter and one near the back—spinning in opposite directions. Others made helicopters with coaxial rotors, or two large rotors sitting atop one another and spinning in opposite directions.

WORLD WAR HELICOPTERS

During World War II, militaries around the world began to realize how helpful the helicopter could be. The United States, France, Germany, Great Britain, and other nations started focusing more time and money on helicopter projects. They wanted helicopters that could carry more weight and fly farther and faster.

However, helicopters still weren't seen much during the war. Germany used some helicopters for antisubmarine warfare, scouting, and carrying supplies. The US military used helicopters mostly for search-and-rescue operations, but not for **combat**. The first US helicopter in service was the Sikorsky R-4 Hoverfly, which the British Royal Navy also used.

US forces used helicopters in India, Burma, and China during World War II.

8

After his success with the VS-300, Igor Sikorsky, pictured on the right, developed the R-4.

The Hoverfly

The Sikorsky R-4 Hoverfly was first used in combat in 1944. It could fly trips of about 130 miles (209 km) and had a top speed of about 75 miles (121 km) per hour. Today, you can see one of these early helicopters at the National Museum of the US Air Force in Ohio.

THE BELL 47

One of the most used helicopters in US history was the Bell 47—military models were also known as the H-13 Sioux. The Bell 47 airlifted about 18,000 **casualties** to mobile army surgical hospitals during the Korean War. These movable hospitals got as close to battle as safety allowed. Some models of the Bell 47 were armed with machine guns, but they were mostly used as airborne ambulances.

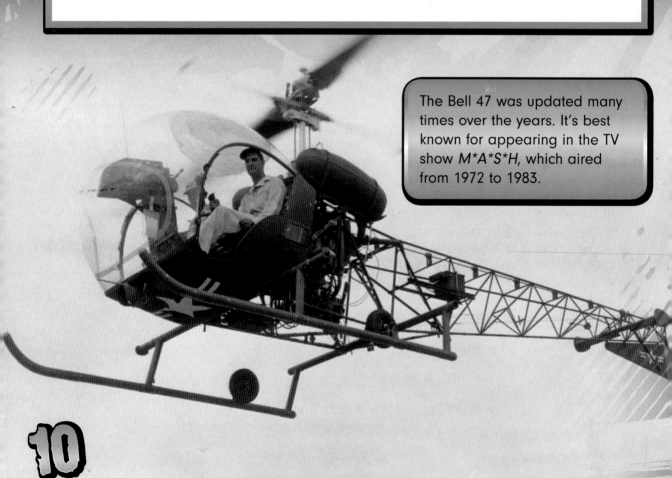

The Bell 47 was updated many times over the years. It's best known for appearing in the TV show *M*A*S*H*, which aired from 1972 to 1983.

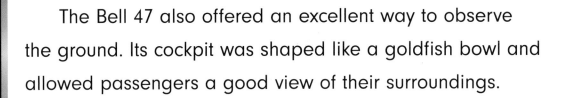

The Bell 47 also offered an excellent way to observe the ground. Its cockpit was shaped like a goldfish bowl and allowed passengers a good view of their surroundings.

This Bell 47 is being used to spray crops in California.

A Popular Way to Fly

The first Bell 47 was produced in the mid-1940s. Over 6,000 had been built when production ended in 1976. Not only was the Bell 47 bought and used by the military, but it was also made to do other tasks. Some models were used for crop dusting, and others delivered mail!

IN VIETNAM

One of the most famous helicopters used during the Vietnam War was the UH-1 Iroquois, more commonly known as the "Huey." More than 16,000 Hueys have been produced since 1960! The Huey proved to be a fast and dependable aircraft for many operations, including transporting troops and search and rescue.

The AH-1 HueyCobra went into service in 1967 during the Vietnam War. It had powerful engines so it could carry weapons. The HueyCobra is considered the first attack helicopter. The latest models of the AH-1, such as the AH-1W SuperCobra, are heavily armed with rockets and **missiles**.

USMC Hueys

Since 1956, the Huey's design has been updated with new technology, though many of its jobs haven't changed. Today, the US Marine Corps still uses Huey models to carry marines and attack enemies at landing areas. Recent Huey models can carry up to eight soldiers along with the helicopter's pilot, copilot, crew chief, and gunner.

The Huey is one of the most successful helicopters ever made. It plays an important role in the armed forces of countries all over the world.

There are many stories of heroic rescues performed by US helicopter pilots in Vietnam. In one rescue, an American pilot was caught in a deep canyon. Enemy soldiers were moving toward him, hoping to capture him.

A helicopter's crew radioed the pilot to remain hidden. They secretly lowered one of the helicopter crewmen down. Then, in sight of the enemy soldiers, they brought the crewman back up. Thinking the US pilot had been rescued, the enemies left! When the enemies were far enough away, the pilot was able to get high enough in the canyon for the helicopter to rescue him.

Helicopters played an important role in the Vietnam War transporting and rescuing soldiers.

During the Vietnam War, troops might have used a rope ladder like this one to climb into a helicopter.

Jungle Rescues

Vietnam has areas covered in thick jungle. This caused trouble for rescue helicopters. The standard cable used to rescue downed pilots got caught in the thick tree branches. A metal seat that folded into a cylinder was created to get through the leaves and branches and down to the pilot on the ground.

15

THE APACHE

The AH-64 Apache Longbow is the US Army's current attack helicopter. The first model of the Apache entered army service in 1984. Two soldiers man the Apache—a pilot and a gunner. The gunner is in charge of the Apache's **radar**-guided missiles, rockets, and a large machine gun.

Apache Technology

To aid it in performing its many tasks, the Apache has advanced onboard electronics. Its computer helps find targets and keeps missiles on course. When flying at night, the Apache has night-vision sensors that use heat to help identify objects around the helicopter.

The Apache is used for several types of operations. Since it's a well-armed and armored helicopter, the Apache is effective at destroying targets behind enemy lines. The Apache is also used for scouting when there's a chance that enemy forces might shoot back. Apache helicopters were used in the conflicts in Iraq and Afghanistan.

The Apache is sometimes called a flying tank because of its armor and weapons.

THE CHINOOK

The US military often uses helicopters to transport troops and supplies. One model currently in use is the CH-47 Chinook. It first entered army service in 1962 and has been improved several times over the years to remain valuable to the military. The latest Chinooks can carry up to 19,500 pounds (8,853 kg)! They're able to transport vehicles inside the helicopter or carry large loads on the outside using a triple-hook system.

The Chinook normally has a crew of three—two pilots and an observer. However, it can carry up to 33 soldiers with all their **equipment**!

Chinook Defenses

Even though the Chinook is commonly used as a transport helicopter, it can protect itself, too. It comes equipped with a missile-approach warner, radar warner, and missile countermeasures. Some Chinooks are outfitted with machine guns for when they may need to fight back.

If the army can't fit cargo inside the Chinook, they carry it under the helicopter!

The Kiowa Warrior helicopter is used by the army for scouting and light attack. It's equipped with the latest technology, allowing it to operate day or night and in poor weather conditions. The Kiowa has a mast above its rotor that contains a thermal-imaging system, laser rangefinder, and a low-light television system to observe its surroundings.

The Kiowa can carry many weapons—such as Stinger antiaircraft missiles—to fire at other aircraft. It may also carry machine guns, rockets, or other missiles for targets at close range. An advanced onboard communications system helps steer bombs to their targets, even bombs fired or dropped by other US military aircraft!

Travel Size

The Kiowa Warrior can be sent anywhere in the world. This helicopter is small enough that it can be transported inside another aircraft! Once the Kiowa is unloaded, it can be ready to fly within minutes. Rotors are unfolded, equipment is reattached, and then it's ready to go.

The US Army started using Kiowa Warriors in 1991.

UH-60

The UH-60 was designed to **replace** the Huey helicopter. All branches of the US military use the UH-60 helicopter for many different tasks. Each branch calls their UH-60 a different name. The army and marines use the UH-60 Black Hawk to transport troops and equipment. They also use it as an attack helicopter, arming it with guns, missiles, or rockets.

The US Air Force calls its model of the UH-60 the HH-60 Pave Hawk. The air force uses this helicopter for the search and rescue of people who are in trouble during both war and peacetime.

Navy and Coast Guard UH-60s

The US Navy uses a UH-60 model they call the MH-60 Seahawk. The Seahawk can be equipped to attack enemy ships or submarines and is also used for search and rescue. The US Coast Guard uses its UH-60, the HH-60 Jayhawk, for search-and-rescue and policing operations.

The Black Hawk is a utility helicopter, meaning it can be used for many different jobs.

23

THE OSPREY

The Osprey is one of the newest US military aircraft. Both the marine corps and the air force fly this tilt-rotor aircraft, which is a cross between an airplane and a helicopter. Its rotors are mounted on its wings.

The special feature of the Osprey is that its wings can rotate, or tilt! This means they can turn so the rotors point up, allowing it to fly like a helicopter and take off and land in a small space. Once in the air, the Osprey can rotate its wings again so the rotors face forward. This allows the Osprey to fly fast and far like an airplane.

CV-22 Osprey

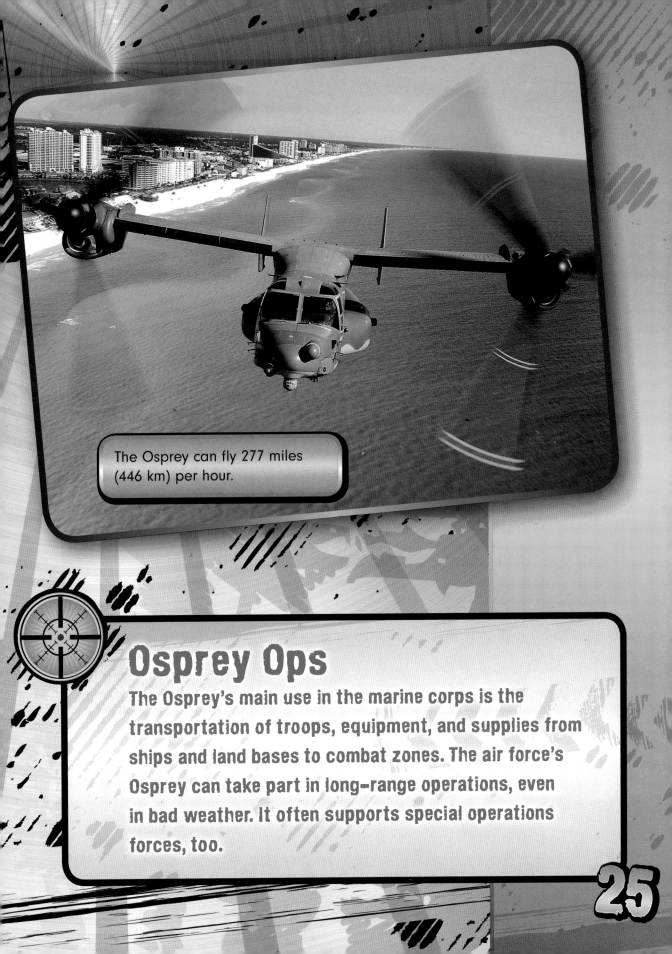

The Osprey can fly 277 miles (446 km) per hour.

Osprey Ops

The Osprey's main use in the marine corps is the transportation of troops, equipment, and supplies from ships and land bases to combat zones. The air force's Osprey can take part in long-range operations, even in bad weather. It often supports special operations forces, too.

TODAY AND TOMORROW

There are many dangers to helicopters flying above the battlefield. Vehicles equipped with large guns can shoot down helicopters if they fly too low. Enemy aircraft equipped with guns and missiles may attack helicopters, too.

Modern helicopters are designed to counter these dangers—and even pose danger themselves! In many cases, helicopter bodies have been made narrower in order to present a smaller target to any guns that might shoot at them. Many now have armor as an added protection as well. Perhaps most importantly, advanced computer systems can often **detect** enemies on the ground and in the air before any weapons are fired.

Heat-Seeking Missiles

Missile systems, such as the US Army's Stinger missiles, can detect heat given off by helicopter engines. These missiles fly faster than any helicopter. However, helicopters can be equipped with special covers for their engines in order to reduce the amount of heat given off.

Helicopters
are important
military tools in
today's conflicts.

The future of American military helicopters will be guided by lessons learned from past helicopters. The military wants to find a way to copy the success and years of service of the dependable UH-1 Huey: a helicopter that can fulfill multiple roles and be effective in those roles for many years. Hueys served the US military and other nations' militaries well for more than 50 years!

Robotic Helicopters

Some helicopters in use today don't even have human pilots in them. In 2012, the US military used robotic helicopters to carry supplies in Afghanistan. These unmanned aircraft can carry 3.5 tons (3.2 mt) of cargo! They can fly very high and at night in order to reduce the risk of being shot down.

Future helicopters will be faster and able to travel farther while carrying a larger load. They must be easy to improve, too, as technology and military equipment advances in the years to come.

The helicopters of tomorrow will be faster and tougher than the helicopters of today.

29

GLOSSARY

casualty: someone who has been hurt or killed

combat: armed fighting between opposing forces

countermeasure: a military system or equipment used to prevent enemy weapons from working

design: to create the pattern or shape of something. Also, the pattern or shape of something.

detect: to notice or discover the existence of something

equipment: tools, clothing, and other items needed for a job

missile: a rocket used to strike something at a distance

radar: a machine that uses radio waves to locate and identify objects

replace: to take the place of something else

rotor: the spinning blades on top of a helicopter that allow it to fly

technology: the practical application of specialized knowledge

torque: a turning or twisting force

vehicle: an object used for carrying or transporting people or goods, such as a car, truck, or airplane

FOR MORE INFORMATION

Books

Abramovitz, Melissa. *Military Helicopters*. Mankato, MN: Capstone Press, 2012.

Alvarez, Carlos. *Army Night Stalkers*. Minneapolis, MN: Bellwether Media, 2010.

David, Jack. *Apache Helicopters*. Minneapolis, MN: Bellwether Media, 2008.

Websites

How Apache Helicopters Work
science.howstuffworks.com/apache-helicopter.htm
Learn more about the Apache helicopter.

U.S. Army Factfiles: Aircraft
www.army.mil/factfiles/equipment/aircraft/index.html
Read about some of the different helicopters the army uses.

Publisher's note to educators and parents: Our editors have carefully reviewed these websites to ensure that they are suitable for students. Many websites change frequently, however, and we cannot guarantee that a site's future contents will continue to meet our high standards of quality and educational value. Be advised that students should be closely supervised whenever they access the Internet.

INDEX